mayores de cuando el hotel era el único. Una niña mulata cantaba boleros de moda, y el mismo Agustín Romero, ya viejo y ciego, la acompañaba bien en el mismo piano de media cola de la fiesta inaugural.

Terminó de prisa, tratando de sobreponerse a la humillación de comer sola, pero se sintió bien con la música, que era suave y sedante, y la niña sabía cantar. Cuando terminó sólo quedaban tres parejas en mesas dispersas, y justo frente a ella un hombre distinto que no había visto entrar. Vestía de lino blanco, con el cabello metálico y el bigote romántico terminado en puntas. Tenía en la mesa una botella de brandy y una copa a la mitad, y parecía estar solo en el mundo.

El piano inició el *Claro de Luna* de Debussy en un aventurado arreglo para bolero, y la niña mulata lo cantó con amor. Conmovida, Ana Magdalena pidió una ginebra con hielo y soda, el único alcohol que se permitía y sobrellevaba bien. Había aprendido a disfrutarla con su esposo, un alegre bebedor social que la trataba con la cortesía y la complicidad de un amante escondido. El mundo cambió desde el primer sorbo. Se

embellecida

ALSO BY GABRIEL GARCÍA MÁRQUEZ

UNTIL AUGUST

GABRIEL GARCÍA
MÁRQUEZ

UNTIL AUGUST

Translated from the Spanish
by Anne McLean

Edited by Cristóbal Pera

ALFRED A. KNOPF
New York | Toronto | 2024

THIS IS A BORZOI BOOK PUBLISHED BY
ALFRED A. KNOPF AND ALFRED A. KNOPF CANADA

All rights reserved. Published in the United States by
Alfred A. Knopf, a division of Penguin Random House LLC,
New York, and in Canada by Alfred A. Knopf Canada, a division
of Penguin Random House Canada Limited, Toronto.

www.aaknopf.com   www.penguinrandomhouse.ca

ISBN: 978-0-593-80199-4 (hardcover)
ISBN: 978-0-593-80200-7 (eBook)
LCCN: 2023947671

Library and Archives Canada Cataloguing in Publication
Title: Until August : a novel / Gabriel García Márquez ; translated by
Anne McLean.
Other titles: En agosto nos vemos. English
Names: García Márquez, Gabriel, 1927–2014, author. | McLean, Anne,
[date] translator.
Description: Translation of: En agosto nos vemos.
Identifiers: Canadiana (ebook) 20230567207 |
Canadiana (print) 20230567193 | ISBN 9781039055742 (EPUB) |
ISBN 9781039055735 (hardcover)
Subjects: LCGFT: Novels.
Classification: LCC PQ8180.17.A73 E5213 2024 | DDC 863/.64—dc23

Jacket photograph by dbtravel/Alamy; (gladiola) by Ron Bull/Alamy
Jacket design by Chip Kidd

Manufactured in the United States of America
1st Printing

CONTENTS

PREFACE

THE MEMORY LOSS OUR FATHER SUFFERED IN his final years, as most people will find easy to imagine, was extremely tough on all of us. But in particular, the way that loss diminished his ability to continue to write with his customary rigor was a source of desperate frustration for him. He told us once with the clarity and eloquence of the great writer he was: "Memory is at once my source material and my tool. Without it, there's nothing."

Until August was the fruit of one last effort to carry on creating against all odds. The process was a race between his artistic perfectionism and his vanishing mental faculties. The lengthy back-and-forth of the many versions of the text is described in detail, much better than we could, by our friend Cristóbal Pera in his editor's note for the Spanish edition. At the time, all we knew was Gabo's final judgment: "This book doesn't work. It must be destroyed."

We did not destroy it, but we did set it aside, in the hope that time would decide what to do with it. Reading it again almost ten years after his death, we discovered that the text contained a great many wonderful achievements. It is not, of course, as polished as his greatest books. It has a few rough patches and contradictions, but nothing that impedes enjoyment of the most outstanding aspects of Gabo's work: his capacity for invention, his poetic use of language, his captivating storytelling, his understanding of humankind, and his affection for our experiences and misadventures, especially when it comes to love. Love, possibly the main subject of his entire oeuvre.

Judging the book to be much better than we remembered it, another possibility occurred to us: that the fading faculties that kept him from finishing the book also kept him from realizing how good it was. In an act of betrayal, we decided to put his readers' pleasure ahead of all other considerations. If they are delighted, it's possible Gabo might forgive us. In that we trust.

—*Rodrigo & Gonzalo García Barcha*

UNTIL AUGUST

1

S HE RETURNED TO THE ISLAND ON FRIDAY, August 16, on the three o'clock ferry. She was wearing jeans, a plaid shirt, plain flat shoes without socks, carrying a satin parasol and a handbag, and her only luggage was a beach bag. In the row of taxis at the dock she went straight to an old model corroded by the sea air. The driver welcomed her warmly and took her jolting across the destitute village, with its mud-walled shacks, palm-thatch roofs, and streets of burning sand beside a sea in flames. He had to swerve around undaunted pigs and naked chil-

dren pretending to be toreadors. On the out-
skirts of the village he drove down an avenue of
royal palms where the beaches and the tourist
hotels were, between the open sea and a lagoon
inhabited by blue herons. At last he stopped
outside the oldest, most dilapidated hotel.

The concierge was waiting for her with the
registration card ready to sign and the keys to
the only room on the second floor that overlooked the lagoon. She climbed the stairs in
four strides and entered the shabby room that
smelled of recent fumigation and was almost
entirely occupied by an enormous double bed.
She took a kidskin toiletry case out of her bag
and a book with uncut pages that she put on the
nightstand with an ivory paper knife marking
her place. She took out a pink silk nightgown
and tucked it under the pillow. She also took out
a silk scarf printed with tropical birds, a short-
sleeved white shirt, and a pair of very worn tennis shoes, and carried them into the bathroom.

Before getting dressed she took off her wedding ring and the men's watch she wore on her

right wrist, put them on the shelf above the sink, and washed her face quickly to get rid of the dust from the journey, scare away the siesta-time fatigue. After she finished drying off she looked in the mirror and appraised her breasts, still round and high in spite of two pregnancies. She stretched her cheeks back with the heels of her hands to remind herself what she'd looked like when young. She ignored the wrinkles on her neck, as there was nothing she could do about them now, and checked her perfect teeth, which she'd brushed after lunch on board the ferry. She rolled deodorant onto her smooth-shaven underarms and put on the fresh cotton shirt with the initials AMB embroidered on the pocket. She brushed her straight black hair, which fell to her shoulders, and tied it up in a ponytail with the bird-print scarf. To complete her look, she rubbed a little vaseline on her lips, moistened her fingertips with her tongue and smoothed down her eyebrows, dabbed a drop of Maderas de Oriente behind each ear, and at last confronted her autumnal, motherly face in the mirror. Her skin without a trace of cosmetics had the color and texture of molasses, and her topaz eyes were beautiful with their dark Portuguese lids. She scrutinized herself thoroughly, judged herself without pity, and found that she looked almost as good as she felt. Only when she put her ring and watch back on did she notice how late she was: it was six minutes to four, but she allowed herself a moment of nostalgia to contemplate the herons that glided in stillness over the steamy torpor of the lagoon.

The taxi was waiting for her beneath the banana thatch at the entrance. Without needing instructions, he drove down the palm-lined avenue to a gap between the hotels where the street market was, and pulled up to a flower stall. A large black woman snoozing in a beach chair was startled awake by the horn, recognized the woman in the back seat of the car, and, laughing and chatting, handed her an already prepared bouquet of gladioli. A few blocks ahead the taxi turned up a barely passable track that climbed along a ridge of sharp stones. Through air crystalized by the heat she could see the wide-open Caribbean, the yachts lined up beside the tourists' dock, the four o'clock ferry on its way back to the city. At the top of the hill was the poorest cemetery. She pushed open the rusty gate without straining and carried the bouquet down the path between burial mounds overgrown with weeds. In the center there was a ceiba tree with huge branches from which she took her bearings to find her mother's grave. The sharp stones hurt her feet through the hot rubber soles of her shoes, and the harsh sun filtered through the satin of her parasol. An iguana emerged from the underbrush, stopped short in front of her, stared for an instant, then scampered away.

She pulled a gardening glove out of her pocket, put it on, and had to clean three gravestones before she recognized the pale marble with her mother's name and the date of her death, eight years earlier.

She had repeated this trip every August 16 at the same time, with the same taxi and the same florist, under the fiery sun of that destitute cemetery, to place a bouquet of fresh gladioli on her mother's grave. After that moment she had nothing to do until nine the next morning, when the first ferry went back to the mainland.

Her name was Ana Magdalena Bach. For twenty-seven of her forty-six years she had been in a well-matched marriage with a man she loved and who loved her and whom she married before finishing her arts-and-letters degree, still a virgin and without any previous relationships. Her mother had been a famous Montessori teacher who, in spite of her talents, never in her entire life wanted to be anything more. Ana Magdalena inherited from her the splendor of her golden eyes, the virtue of being a woman of few words, and the intelligence to manage her temper. They were a family of musicians. Her father had been a piano teacher and the director of the provincial conservatory for forty years. Her husband, an orchestra conductor, also the child of musicians, replaced his teacher when he retired. Ana Magdalena and her husband had an exemplary son who was the first cello of the National Symphony Orchestra by the age of twenty-two, and had been applauded by Mstislav Leopoldovich Rostropovich in a private session. Then there was their eighteen-year-old daughter, who had an almost genius ability to learn any instrument by ear but liked to use it only as a pretext to avoid sleeping at home. She was in the first flush of a fling with an excellent jazz trumpeter but was determined to take her vows with the Discalced Carmelites, against her parents' will.

Three days before she died Ana Magdalena's mother had expressed her wish to be buried on the island. Ana Magdalena had wanted to travel to the funeral, but no one thought it prudent, for she herself did not believe she would survive her grief. Her father took her to the island on the first anniversary to place a marble stone on the grave. The crossing, almost four hours in a canoe with an outboard motor, without a single instant of calm water, frightened her. She admired the golden sand beaches bordered by virgin jungle, the clamor of birdsong, and the

phantasmal flight of the herons above the stillness of the lagoon. She was depressed by the
poverty of the village, where they had to sleep
outside in hammocks slung between two coconut palms, despite its being the birthplace of
a poet and a grandiloquent senator who had
once very nearly been president of the republic.
She was struck by the number of black fisher-
men with mutilated arms from the premature
explosions of dynamite sticks. However, she
understood her mother's wish when she saw
the splendor of the world from the height of the
cemetery. It was the only solitary place where
one could not feel alone. That was when Ana
Magdalena Bach decided to leave her mother
there where she lay and assigned herself the
task of bringing a bouquet of gladioli every year
to place on her grave.

August was the month of heat waves and
crazy downpours, but she understood it as yet
another penance she must fulfill unfailingly and
always alone. Her only weakness came in the
face of her children's insistence on seeing their

grandmother's grave, and nature made her pay with a terrifying crossing. The motorboat set sail despite the rain so night would not fall on the way and the children arrived petrified and overcome with seasickness. That time, fortunately, they were able to sleep in the first tourist hotel the senator built in his name with state funding.

Ana Magdalena Bach had seen more towering cliffs of glass go up every year while the village grew more and more impoverished. The ferry replaced the motorboats. The crossing still took four hours, but with air-conditioning, a band, and pleasure girls. She alone maintained her routine as the village's most punctual visitor.

She went back to the hotel, lay down on the bed wearing nothing but her lace panties, opened her book to the page marked by the paper knife, and began to read beneath the blades of a ceiling fan that barely stirred the heat. The book was *Dracula*, by Bram Stoker. On the ferry she had raced with fervor through the first half of the masterpiece but this time fell asleep with the book on her chest. She woke up two hours later in darkness, drenched in sweat and starving.

The hotel bar was open until ten, and before going back to sleep she went down to eat whatever was on offer. She noticed there were more clients than usual at that hour, and the waiter didn't seem to be the same one who had been there before. To avoid complications she ordered the same toasted ham and cheese sandwich as in previous years, and a coffee with milk. While they were bringing it she realized she was surrounded by the same older tourists as when this hotel had been the only one. A young woman was singing sad boleros and Agustín Romero himself, now old and blind, accompanied her lovingly on the same decrepit piano from the inaugural fiesta.

She ate her food quickly, trying to overcome the humiliation of eating alone, but she felt good listening to the music, which was soft and tranquil, and the girl could sing. When she finished there were only three couples left at scattered tables and, right in front of her, a man she hadn't seen come in. He wore a white linen suit and had silver hair. There was a bottle of brandy on his table and a half-empty glass, and he looked as if he was alone in the world.

The piano began a daring bolero arrangement of Debussy's "Clair de lune," and the girl sang it with love. Moved, Ana Magdalena Bach ordered a gin with ice and soda, the only alcohol that agreed with her. The world changed with her first sip. She felt mischievous, joyful, capable of anything, and beautified by the sacred mixture of music and gin. She thought the man at the table in front of hers had not seen her, but she caught him watching her when she looked at him a second time. He blushed. She held his gaze while he looked at his pocket watch. He put it away in embarrassment, refilled his glass, one eye on the door, bewildered, because he was now aware that she was staring at him without mercy. Then he looked straight at her. She smiled and he greeted her with a slight nod.

"May I offer you a drink?" he asked.

"That would be a pleasure," she said.

He moved to her table and very stylishly poured her a shot. "Cheers," he said. She perked up, and they both knocked back their drinks in one. He choked, coughed with his whole body shuddering, and was left with tears streaming down his face. They were silent for a long moment while he dried off with a lavender-scented handkerchief and recovered his voice. She dared to ask him if he was expecting anyone.

"No," he said. "There was something important but it didn't work out."

She asked with an expression of calculated incredulity: "Business?" He answered: "I'm no good for anything else anymore." But he said it in the tone of voice men use when they don't want to be believed. She obliged him, and added a tasteless comment far from her normal way of being but well judged:

"That may be what they tell you at home."

And so she carried on shepherding him with

her delicate touch, until she had him roped into banal chitchat. She tried to guess his age, and was one year over: forty-six. She tried to guess his country of origin from his accent, and after three tries gave up: he was a Hispanic gringo. She tried to guess his profession, and after her second attempt he hastened to tell her he was a civil engineer, which she suspected was a ruse to prevent her from stumbling onto the truth.

She talked about the audacity of turning a Debussy piece into a bolero, but he hadn't noticed. No doubt he realized that she knew about music, whereas he hadn't gone beyond "The Blue Danube." She told him she was reading Stoker's *Dracula*. He had read it in school, and was still struck by the episode of the count disembarking in London transformed into a dog. She agreed, and did not understand why Francis Ford Coppola had changed it in his unforgettable film. After the second drink she felt that the brandy had met up with the gin in some corner of her heart, and she had to concentrate in order not to lose her head. The music ended at eleven and the band was only waiting for them to leave so they could close.

She knew him by then as if she had always lived with him. She knew he was clean, impeccably dressed, with inexpressive hands accentuated by the natural shine of his fingernails, and with a good and cowardly heart. She realized that he was ill at ease under the gaze of her big golden eyes and did not take them off him. Then she felt bold enough to take a step that had never occurred to her in her entire life, not even in dreams, and she took it without any mystique:

"Shall we go up?"

He was at a loss.

"I'm not staying here," he said.

But she did not even wait for him to finish his sentence. "I am," she said. She stood up and shook her head a little to get it under control. "Second floor, number 203, to the right of the stairs. Don't knock, just come right in."

She went up to her room feeling a delicious terror she had not experienced since her wedding night. She turned on the ceiling fan but not the light, undressed in the darkness right away, and left a trail of clothing on the floor from the door to the bathroom. When she turned on the vanity light she had to close her eyes and inhale deeply to control her breathing and the trembling of her hands. She had a quick wash between her legs, under her arms, and between her toes, which had marinated in her rubber-soled shoes. Despite sweating all afternoon, she hadn't planned to shower until the next morning. There was no time to brush her teeth so she put a tiny bit of toothpaste on her tongue and went back to the bedroom illuminated only by the bathroom's oblique beam.

She did not wait for her guest to push on the door, but pulled it open from inside when she heard him approaching. He was startled, but she did not give him time for anything else in the darkness. She yanked off his jacket, his tie, his shirt, and threw them over her shoulder onto the floor. As she did so, the air filled with the faint scent of lavender. The man tried to help her at first, but she didn't give him time. When she had him naked to the waist she sat him down on the bed and knelt down to take off his shoes and socks. He unbuckled his belt at the same time and unbuttoned his fly, so she just had to tug his trousers to get them off. Neither of them worried about the keys and cash and coins and pocketknife that spilled across the floor. Finally, she helped him to slide his shorts down his legs, and noticed that he was not as well endowed as her husband, who was the only adult she'd ever seen naked, but he was serene and upstanding.

She did not allow him any initiative. She straddled him, took him in right up to her soul and devoured him for her own pleasure not even thinking of his, until they were both left perplexed and exhausted in a soup of sweat. She stayed on top, struggling against the first pangs of her conscience beneath the suffocating noise of the ceiling fan, until she noticed that he was having trouble breathing plastered under the weight of her body, his arms outstretched, and she rolled onto her back beside him. He remained still until he caught his breath enough to ask:

"Why me?"

"It was a flash of inspiration," she said.

"Coming from a woman like you," he said, "that's an honor."

"Ah," she joked: "Was it not a pleasure?"

He did not answer, and they both lay listening intently to the sounds of their souls. The room was beautiful in the green shadows of the lagoon. They heard wingbeats. He asked: "What's that?" She told him about the habits of night herons. After a long hour of idle whispering she began to explore with her fingers, very slowly, from his chest down to his lower belly. She continued touching his legs with her toes, and discovered that his whole body was covered in thick soft hair like April moss. Then she reached again for the resting creature and found it deflated but alive. He made it easier with a change of position. She surveyed him with her fingertips: the size, the shape, the palpitating frenulum, the silky glans, topped off with a little fold that felt like it had been sewn with baling needles. She counted the stitches by touch, and he hastened to tell her what she had imagined: "I was circumcised as an adult." And he added with a sigh:

"It was a very strange pleasure."

"At least," she said mercilessly, "it wasn't an honor."

She hastened to mitigate the blow with gentle kisses on his ear, on his neck; he searched for her mouth and they kissed on the lips for the first time. She reached for him again, and found him ready. She wanted to attack, but he revealed himself to be an exquisite lover who raised her unhurriedly to the boiling point. She was surprised that such inexpressive hands could be capable of such tenderness and tried to resist flirtatiously. But he asserted himself firmly, handled her his own way, and made her happy.

It was after two when a thunderclap shook the foundations of the building and the wind unlatched the window. She rushed to close it, and in the instantaneous high noon of another lightning flash she saw the choppy lagoon and, through the rain, an immense moon on the horizon and blue herons flapping their wings in an airless squall. He slept.

On her way back to bed her feet got tangled in both their clothes. She left hers on the floor to pick up later, and hung his jacket over the back of the chair, his shirt and tie on top of it, folded his trousers carefully to preserve the crease without wrinkling them, and placed his keys, knife, and money on top of them. The storm had cooled the air in the room a little, so she put on her pink nightgown made of silk so pure it tingled her skin. The man, asleep on his side with his legs tucked up, looked to her like an enormous orphan, and she could not help but feel a burst of compassion. She lay down behind him, wrapped her arm around his waist, and the warmth of her drenched body soon woke him up. He let out a rasping breath and pulled away in his sleep. She barely slept, and

woke up in the sudden quiet when the electricity went off and the room, without the fan, was
left in a steamy semi-darkness. He was snoring by then with a continuous wheeze. Out of
simple mischief, she began to fondle him with
her fingertips. He stopped snoring with a start
and began to come back to life. She abandoned
him for an instant to pull her silk nightgown
off. But when she got back to him her artistry
was in vain, as she noticed he was pretending to
sleep so he wouldn't have to indulge her a third
time. She put her nightgown back on and went
to sleep with her back to him.

Her internal clock woke her at six. She
lay there drifting for a moment with her eyes
closed, not daring to admit the pulsing pain
at her temples, or the icy nausea, or the anxiety about something unknown that no doubt
awaited her in real life. From the noise of the
fan she realized that the electricity was back on
and the bedroom must already be visible in the
blue dawn of the lagoon. All of a sudden, like a
fatal flash, she was struck by the brutal aware-

ness that, for the first time in her life, she had fornicated and spent the night with a man who was not her own. She turned in fright to look at him over her shoulder, and he was not there. Nor was he in the bathroom. She turned on the lights and saw that his clothes were gone, and instead hers, which she'd left strewn across the floor, were folded and placed almost lovingly on the chair. Only then did she realize she knew nothing about him, not even his name, and all that was left of her wild night was the sad scent of lavender in the air purified by the storm. Only when she picked up her book from the bedside table to put it in her bag did she notice that he had left between its pages of horror a twenty-dollar bill.

2

SHE WOULD NEVER BE THE SAME. SHE'D caught a glimpse of him on the ferry going back, among the hordes of tourists toward whom she had always been indifferent and all of a sudden and without clear reasons found loathsome. She had always been a good reader. Having left university just a few courses short of a literature degree, she had read with rigor what she had to read, and went on reading what she liked best: love stories by well-known authors, the longer and more ill-fated the better. She spent several years reading short novels of many genres, such as *The Old Man and the Sea, Lazarillo de Tormes,* and *The Stranger*. She detested fashionable books and knew that time would never allow her to keep up to date. In recent years she had delved deeply into supernatural novels. But that day she stretched out in the sun on deck and could not read a single letter, or think of anything other than the previous night.

The buildings of the port, so narrow and so familiar since her school days, seemed alien and rotted by the salty sea air. At the dock she took a public bus as decrepit as those from her childhood, crammed with poor people and with the radio at carnival volume, but this particular bus on that stifling day at noon seemed to her more uncomfortable than ever, and for the first time she was annoyed by the bad moods and farmyard stink of her fellow passengers. The tumultuous market bazaars, which she'd claimed as her own since she was a little girl and where just the previous week she had been shopping with her daughter without the slightest fear, made her shudder as if she were in the streets of Calcutta, where gangs of garbage collectors used sticks to hit the bodies lying on the sidewalks at dawn, to find out which ones were sleeping and which were dead. At the Rotonda de la Independencia she saw the equestrian statue of the Liberator unveiled thirty years earlier, and only that day did she notice that the horse was rearing up and the sword wielded against the sky.

When she got home, in a panic she asked Filomena, their lifelong housekeeper, what disaster had occurred in her absence to keep the birds from singing in their cages and why her planters of flowers from the Amazon, hanging baskets of ferns, and garlands of blue vines had disappeared from the inside courtyard. Filomena reminded her that she'd taken them out to the patio to enjoy the rain, just as Ana Magdalena had instructed before she left. However, it would take several days before Ana Magdalena became aware that the changes were not to the world but to herself. She had always gone through life without looking at it, and only that year upon her return from the island did she begin to see it with chastened eyes.

She did not know why she'd changed, but it had something to do with the twenty-dollar bill she carried around at page 116 of her book. She had suffered unbearable humiliation, without a moment's serenity. She had wept with rage from the frustration of not knowing the identity of the man she would have to kill for debasing the memory of a happy adventure. During the ferry crossing she felt at peace with herself over a loveless act that she designated for her conscience as a private matter between herself and her husband, but she could not overcome her resentment at the bill she sensed burning like a live coal, less in her purse than in her heart. She did not know whether to frame it as a trophy or tear it to shreds to exorcise the indignity. The only thing that seemed indecent was to spend it.

The day was further ruined when Filomena told her that her husband still wasn't up at two o'clock in the afternoon. She didn't remember that ever happening before, except for the few Saturdays they stayed up all night together and spent entire Sundays in bed. She found him laid out with a headache. He had left the curtains open and the blinding afternoon light reverberated inside the bedroom. She closed them and was about to rouse her husband with an affectionate greeting but was prevented by a gloomy thought. Almost without thinking she asked him the question she most feared:

"Might I know where you were last night?"

He looked at her in shock. That question, extremely common even in happy marriages, had never been heard in their house. More amused than worried, he asked her in turn: "Where or with whom?" She put up her guard: "What do you mean by that?" But he eluded the challenge and told her he'd had a splendid night listening to jazz with their daughter Micaela. He immediately changed the subject:

"By the way," he said. "You haven't even told me how your trip went."

She thought in alarm that her inappropriate question might have stirred the ashes of some ancient suspicion. The mere idea terrified her. "Same as ever," she said. "The power went off in the hotel and in the morning there was no water in the shower," she lied, "so I've been sweating for two days and haven't washed. But the sea was calm and cool and I was able to snooze here and there on the way back."

He leapt out of bed, in his underwear, as he always slept, and went to the bathroom. He was huge, athletic, and gracefully handsome. She followed him, and they continued their conversation, he from the steamed-up shower cubicle and she sitting on the toilet lid, as they had done since they were newlyweds. She slid back to the subject of their unruly daughter. She was named Micaela after her grandmother who was buried on the island, and she was stubbornly determined to become a nun, even while she carried on with a slightly older virtuoso jazz musician, with whom she stayed out partying until dawn. Her mother did not understand it, but that afternoon she was more baffled by why her daughter was willing to be seen with her father in a dive bar full of stoned musicians. Her husband teased her cheerfully:

"Don't tell me you're spying on me with our own daughter."

It would have been a relief for her to say yes, but she realized in time that it wasn't a good day to embitter their loving banter. He hummed the first bars of the Grieg piano concerto as he lathered up under the shower. All of a sudden he turned around.

"Aren't you coming in?"

She had a single reason to hesitate, and for someone as scrupulous as her it was a weighty reason.

"I haven't washed since yesterday," she said. "I stink."

"All the more reason," he said. "The water feels wonderful."

She took off the plaid shirt, jeans, and lace panties she'd worn on her trip back from the island, threw them in the laundry hamper, and stepped into the shower. He gave her his place under the water and soaped her up as usual, from her feet to her head, without interrupting the conversation.

It wasn't anything new. They had been able to hold on to certain intimacies, and one of those was showering together. At first they did it because they both started work at the same time, and instead of the classic eternal dispute over who should shower first, they learned to do it together. They lathered each other up with so much affection that they often ended up rolling around on the bathroom floor, on a silk bathmat that she'd bought to avoid destroying her back in the throes of passion.

During the first three years it was like clock-work every day, at night in bed or in the morning in the bathroom, except for the sacred truces during her periods and after childbirth.

In time they both foresaw the threat of routine, and without even discussing it they decided to add a touch of adventure to their love. They started to go to assignation motels, sometimes the most refined but just as often the sleaziest, until one night when the place was robbed at gunpoint and they were left stark naked. The mood would strike them at such unexpected moments that she started carrying condoms in her purse to avoid surprises. Then they discovered by chance a brand with its advertising slogan printed on the packet: *Next Time Buy Lutecian*. This inaugurated a long stage in which each act of love would be rewarded with a felicitous phrase, from obscene jokes to Seneca's maxims.

With the arrival of the children and the demands of their schedules, their pace slowed, but they picked it up again whenever they could. It was always a joyful love where even madness was admissible. Even in their lowest moments they devised ways to renew their passion, until they came full circle and got back into their old routine again.

His name was Doménico Amarís. Fifty-four years old, well educated, handsome, and refined, he'd been the director of the provincial conservatory for over twenty years. In addition to his excellent qualifications as a teacher he was a charmer and such a talented musical caricaturist that he could save a party with a bolero by Agustín Lara in the style of Chopin, or a Cuban danzón in the manner of Rachmaninoff. He had been university champion of everything: singing, swimming, public speaking, table tennis. Nobody told a joke better than he did, or knew every obscure dance from the contradanza to the Charleston and the apache tango. He was a daring conjurer who once at a gala dinner at the conservatory made a live, flapping chicken emerge from the soup tureen at the moment the governor took the lid off to serve. No one knew he played chess until the night he challenged Paul Badura-Skoda after a glorious concert and they drew eleven matches, playing until nine the next morning. His career as a prankster nearly culminated in catastrophe when he convinced the García twins to exchange fiancés, who were each about to marry a bride that wasn't his own. It was his last practical joke, because neither the bridegrooms nor anyone from either family ever forgave him. Nevertheless, Ana Magdalena had adapted to him, become like him, and they knew each other so well deep down that they ended up seeming like one and the same.

He felt he was at the top of his game, full of original ideas. He had always thought that the work of great musicians was inseparable from their destinies, and believed he had proved it through systematic study of the music and lives of the great masters. He thought Brahms's most inspired work was his concerto for violin and could not understand how he had not also composed a masterful concerto for cello, as Dvořák eventually did. He gave up conducting the orchestra and stopped listening to recorded music, preferring to read it, except in the case of a very rare performance. The experimental workshops he ran at the provincial conservatory were enough for him.

With these perhaps indemonstrable opinions of his own, he was writing a manual for a new, more human way of listening to music, and a different heart for performing it. He was deep into chapters on his three major examples: Mozart and Schubert, torrential geniuses with short and troubled lives, and Chausson, victim of an absurd bicycle accident when he was at the height of his powers.

The only family worry, in reality, was the behavior of their daughter, Micaela, a charming hothead. She was still stubbornly trying to convince her parents that being a nun in these times was not the same as before, and she was sure that at the dawn of the third millennium they would even do away with the vow of chastity. The strangest thing was that her mother opposed her vocation for reasons different from her father's. For him it was a matter of little importance as there were already more than enough musicians in the family. Ana Magdalena herself had tried to learn to play the trumpet, but could not. The whole family knew how to sing. But in the case of their daughter, the problem was that she had acquired the happy custom of not sleeping at night. The situation reached a crisis when she disappeared for an entire weekend with her mixed-race trumpet player. They did not resort to the police because among her young bohemian crowd there wasn't a single friend who didn't know where they were. So: they were on the island. Her mother suffered an attack of delayed terror. Micaela tried to placate her with the unexpected news that she had taken a rose to lay on her grandmother's grave. They never knew if this was true, and Ana Magdalena had no desire to find out. She simply informed Micaela that she should have consulted her for a reason her daughter could not have known. Ana Magdalena explained:

"Mamá hated roses."

Doménico Amarís understood his daughter's reasons, but did not contradict his wife out of loyalty, and as ever in such situations remained neutral. Fortunately Micaela agreed that, for several months, she would not stay out all night except on weekends. She often ate with the family, spent up to three hours a day on the phone, and then shut herself up in her room after dinner watching movies on television, which emitted screams and explosions that made the household endure a long night of horror. To the further bewilderment of her parents, during dinner table conversations she showed signs of an active, informed, and mature grasp of current and cultural affairs. Even more: by chance her mother discovered that the endless phone calls were not with the jazz boyfriend but with an official catechist of the Discalced Carmelites, and she celebrated that as a lesser evil.

That's how things stood one night at dinner when Ana Magdalena revealed her fear that her daughter would come back pregnant from one of her weekends, and Micaela tried to reassure her with the good news that a doctor friend had implanted her with a foolproof device when she was fifteen. Her mother, who had never dared go any further than illustrated condoms, was beside herself and shouted straight from the heart:

"Whore!"

The silence after the shout remained vitrified for several days in the air of the house. Ana Magdalena wept inconsolably, locked in her room, more from shame at her own impetuousness than malice against her daughter. Her husband behaved as if he did not exist while his wife was crying, for by then he knew that the reasons for her tears were only within her, though he did not know what they were.

His concern frightened her and underlined what seemed to be men's new attitude toward her. She had always been besieged with offers, yet she was so indifferent to them that she ignored them without pity. However, that year, after returning from the island, she felt as if she had a stigmata on her forehead, visible only to men, a mark that could not go unnoticed by someone who loved her so much and whom she loved more than anyone else. They had both been hardened smokers of two packs a day for many years and had agreed to quit together in solidarity. But she relapsed after coming back from the island. He noticed the ashtrays being moved from their usual places, the odd carelessly forgotten butt, and detected the smell of tobacco in spite of her stealthy fumigation with air fresheners.

Everything changed after she returned from the island. She spent several months without turning a page of Borges, Bioy, and Ocampo's anthology, *The Book of Fantasy*. She slept badly, sneaking off to the bathroom in the early hours to smoke and flushing the toilet to get rid of the floating evidence he knew he would find when he got up at five. She didn't get up just to smoke, but the opposite: she smoked because she was not at peace enough to sleep. Sometimes she turned on the light to read for a few minutes, turned it off again, tossed and turned in bed with pinpoint precision to avoid waking her husband. Until he dared to ask her: "What is going on with you?" She answered dryly:

"Nothing. Why?"

"Forgive me," he said, "but it's impossible for me not to notice how different you've become." And he rounded it off with his exquisite tact: "Have I done something wrong?"

"I don't know, because I hadn't even noticed myself," she said, with a steadiness that astonished her husband. "But maybe you're right. Could it be this nightmare with Micaela?"

"It started before that," he said and dared to take the final step: "You came back from the island like this."

With the first heat waves of July, she began to feel butterfly wings in her chest that would give her no respite until she returned to the island. It was a long month, made longer still by the uncertainty. It had always been a trip as simple as a Sunday at the beach, but that year it was dominated by panic about whether she would meet her fleeting twenty-dollar lover, whom in her heart she had already repudiated.

Instead of the jeans and beach bag of previous years she wore a two-piece ecru linen suit and gold sandals, and packed a case with a formal gown, high-heeled shoes, and a set of faux emerald jewelry. She felt like a different woman: renewed and capable.

3

⸺

WHEN SHE DISEMBARKED ON THE ISLAND she saw her taxi was more dilapidated than ever and decided to take a new, air-conditioned one. Since she didn't know any of the hotels apart from the one she always stayed at, she instructed the driver to take her to the new Carlton, a precipice of gold-tinted glass she had watched going up among the iron crags on her last three visits. It was not possible to find a room she could afford in the August high season, but they gave her a discount on an ice-cold suite on the eighteenth floor that overlooked the circular horizon of the Caribbean and the immense lagoon as far as the mountains. The price was a quarter of her monthly teacher's salary, but the splendor, the silence, the spring-time climate of the vestibule, and the solicitude of the staff infused her with a feeling of security that she surely owed herself.

From three thirty in the afternoon, when she arrived, until eight o'clock that night, when she went down for dinner, she did not have a moment of calm. The gladioli at the hotel's flower shop looked splendid, but they were ten times the price, so she settled for the florist from her last couple of visits. The florist was the first to warn her about the new tourist cemetery, which was advertised as a garden of native flowers with music and birds at the edge of the lagoon but in which they buried the bodies vertically to save space.

She arrived at the island cemetery after five, when it was less sunny than in other years. Some of the tombs had been emptied, and beside them lay the debris of shattered coffins and odd bones among piles of quicklime. In her last-minute haste she'd forgotten her gardening gloves and had to clear the grave with her bare hands while giving her mother a summary of the year. The only good news belonged to her son, who in December would have his debut as a soloist in the Philharmonic Orchestra with Tchaikovsky's *Variations on a Rococo Theme*. She performed miracles to save her daughter's reputation without mentioning her religious vocation, which would not have endeared her to her mother. Finally, she tightened her heart into a fist and confided to her mother the tale of her previous year's night of free love, which she had reserved just for her, and just for that moment. She told her she knew neither who he was nor what his name might be. She was so convinced that her mother would send her a sign of approval that she expected it instantly. She looked up at the ceiba in flower, its repeated clusters blowing in the wind; she saw the sky, the sea, the Miami-bound plane more than an hour behind schedule in the incessant sky.

When she got back to the hotel she felt embarrassed by the state of her clothes and dust-covered hair. She hadn't been to the hairdresser's for a year, since her hair was fine and manageable, and she had adapted to its character. A pedantic and fawning stylist, who should have been called Narciso rather than Gastón, received her with all sorts of tempting suggestions about her hair's possibilities, and ended up giving her a sort of grande dame chignon like she did herself (with less rhetoric) for her society evenings. A maternal manicurist repaired her hands with vanity balm after their battles with the cemetery stubble, and she felt so good that she promised to return the following year on the same date and attempt a change of style. Gastón explained they would charge it to her hotel bill, apart from the ten percent tip. And how much would that be?

"Twenty dollars," Gastón said.

She twitched at the inconceivable coincidence that could only be the sign she was expecting from her mother to cauterize the aftereffects of her adventure. She took out the bill that had been burning in the bottom of her purse all year like the eternal flame of the unknown lover and handed it to the hairstylist with delight.

"Spend it well," she said happily: "It comes from flesh and blood."

Other mysteries of that extravagant hotel were not so easy for Ana Magdalena Bach. When she lit a cigarette she set off a system of bells and lights, and an authoritarian voice told her in three languages that she was in a non-smoking room. She had to ask for help to discover that the same card that opened the door also turned on the lights, the television, the air-conditioning, and the ambient music. She was shown what to type on the electronic keyboard of the round bathtub to regulate the erotic and clinical settings of the jacuzzi. Mad with curiosity she took off her clothes, which were drenched in sweat from the sun at the cemetery, put on the shower cap to protect her hairstyle, and surrendered herself to the whirlpool of foam. Happy, she dialed her home telephone number, and shouted the truth to her husband: "You can't imagine how much I miss you." Her boasting was so vivid, he felt her arousal right down the phone line.

"Damn," he said, "you owe me one."

When she went down for supper it was eight. She thought of ordering something to eat by phone so she wouldn't have to get dressed, but the charge for room service convinced her to eat downstairs in the café like one of the masses. The black silk sheath dress, too long to be in fashion, went well with her hairstyle. She felt slightly helpless with the neckline, but the necklace, earrings, and rings with faux emeralds raised her morale and magnified the brilliance of her eyes.

She finished her ham and cheese sandwich and coffee quickly. Overwhelmed by the shouts of tourists and strident music, she decided to go up to her room to read John Wyndham's *The Day of the Triffids*, which she'd been meaning to get to for more than three months. The calm of the lobby revived her, and as she passed the cabaret a couple of professionals caught her attention dancing to the "Emperor Waltz" with perfect technique. She stood in the doorway, absorbed, even after the couple finished their exhibition and the dance floor was invaded by the regular clientele. A soft, virile voice close behind her woke her from her daydream:

"Shall we dance?"

He was so close that she could pick up the tenuous scent of his fear behind his aftershave. Then she looked at him over her shoulder and gasped. "Sorry," she said in a daze, "but I'm not dressed for dancing." The reply was instantaneous:

"You are the one wearing the dress, señora."

The phrase impressed her. With an unconscious gesture she patted her body with the palms of her hands, her clear chest, pert breasts, bare arms, to make sure that her body really was where she felt it to be. Then she looked at him again over her shoulder, now not to see the owner of the voice but to take possession of him with the most beautiful eyes he would ever see.

"You are so kind," she said charmingly. "Men don't say things like that anymore."

Then he stepped up beside her and reiterated in silence, with a languid hand, his invitation to dance. Ana Magdalena Bach, alone and free on her island, gripped that hand as if it were the edge of a precipice, with all her body's energy. They danced three waltzes in the old style. She assumed from the first steps, judging by the cynicism of his mastery, that he was another professional contracted to brighten up the tourists' nights, and she allowed herself to be swept around in circles of flight, but she kept him firmly at arm's length. He said, looking into her eyes: "You dance like an artist." She knew it was true, but then she knew he would have said it in any case to any woman he wanted to take to bed. During the second waltz he tried to hold her tight against his body, and she kept him in his place. He took the hint and upped his game, guiding her by the waist with his fingertips, like a flower. She responded as an equal. Midway through the third waltz she knew him as if she always had.

Never had she imagined so handsome a man with such an antiquated look. His skin was pale, his eyes ardent beneath luxuriant brows, his jet-black hair slicked down with a perfect center part. His tropical ecru silk dinner jacket tight around his narrow ribs completed the image of a dandy. Everything about him was as false as his manners, but his feverish eyes looked eager for compassion.

At the end of the series of waltzes he led her to a secluded table without warning or per-mission. It was not necessary: she anticipated everything and was delighted when he ordered champagne. The dimly lit ballroom was made for pleasure, and each table had its own atmo-sphere of intimacy. They rested during a ses-sion of salsa, watching the frenzied couples, because she knew that he had only one thing to say to her. It was quick. They drank half a bottle of champagne. The salsas finished at eleven, and a fanfare announced a special presentation by Elena Burke, the bolero queen, exclusive and for one night only on her triumphant tour of the Caribbean. And there she was, dazzled by the lights amid thunderous applause.

Ana Magdalena reckoned the man was not over thirty, because he could barely lead a bolero. She guided him with serene tact, and he picked up the steps. She kept him at a distance, not for decorum this time, but so as not to give him the pleasure of feeling the blood in her veins feverish from the champagne. But he forced her, gently at first, and then with all the strength of his arm around her waist. Then she felt on her thigh what he had wanted her to feel to mark his territory. She sensed the weakness in her knees and cursed herself for the beating of the blood in her veins and the impossible heat of her breathing. However, she managed to pull herself together and refused a second bottle of champagne. He must have noticed, as he invited her for a stroll on the beach. She hid her displeasure with a compassionate frivolity:

"Do you know how old I am?"

"I can't imagine you are any age," he said. "Just as old as you want to be."

He hadn't finished speaking when she, fed up with so many lies, delivered an ultimatum to her body: now or never. "I'm sorry," she said as she stood up, "I have to go." He leapt up in confusion.

"What happened?"

"I have to go," she said. "Champagne doesn't really agree with me."

He suggested other innocent plans, perhaps not knowing that when a woman leaves there is no human or divine power that can stop her. He finally gave in.

"Will you allow me to accompany you?"

"Don't bother," she said. "And thank you, really, for an unforgettable night."

In the elevator she was already regretting it. She felt a ferocious self-loathing. But it was offset by the pleasure of having done the right thing. She walked into the room, took off her shoes, flopped onto her back on the bed, and lit a cigarette. The smoke alarms went off. Almost at the same moment there was a knock on the door, and she cursed the hotel where the law persecuted guests even in the privacy of the bathroom. But it wasn't the law knocking at the door, it was him. He looked like a figure from a wax museum in the semidarkness of the corridor. She stood staring at him with her hand on the doorknob, without a pinch of indulgence, and finally let him in. He strode in as if into his own home.

"Offer me something," he said.

"Help yourself," she said breezily. "I don't have the slightest idea how this spaceship works."

He, however, knew it all. He dimmed the lights, put on some ambient music, and poured two glasses of champagne from the minibar with the mastery of a stage director. She went along with the game, not as herself but as the protagonist of her own narrative. They were drinking a toast when the phone rang. She answered. A hotel security officer explained very kindly that nobody could be in a suite after midnight without registering at reception.

"You don't have to explain, please," she interrupted, embarrassed. "Forgive me."

She hung up the phone, her face bright red. As if he'd heard the warning, he explained it away with a facile reason: "They're Mormons." And without further ado he invited her to the beach to watch the total lunar eclipse in an hour and fifteen minutes. This was news to her. She had a childish passion for eclipses, but all night she had been struggling between decorum and temptation, and could not find a valid argument to make up her mind.

"There is no escape," he said. "It's our destiny."

The supernatural invocation dispensed with her scruples. So they went in his luxurious camper van to watch the eclipse from a tiny bay hidden in a grove of coconut palms with no sign of tourists. On the horizon they could

see the distant brilliance of the city, and the sky
was diaphanous and full of stars, with a sad and
solitary moon. He parked in the shelter of the
palm trees, took off his shoes, loosened his belt,
and reclined his seat to relax. Only then did she
discover that the vehicle didn't have any seats
apart from the two front ones, which turned
into beds at the flip of a switch. The rest was a
tiny bar, a stereo system playing the saxophone
music of Fausto Papetti, and a minuscule bathroom with a portable bidet behind a crimson
curtain. She understood instantly.

"There won't be an eclipse," she said.

He gave his word that he had heard it on the
news.

"No," she said. "You can only have an eclipse
when the moon is full, and we've got a waxing
quarter crescent."

He remained imperturbable.

"Then it must be solar," he said. "That gives
us more time."

There were no more formalities. They both
now knew what they were doing, and she knew

it was all she could have expected from him since they danced that first bolero. She was astonished by the magician's mastery with which he removed her clothes piece by piece, his fingertips barely touching her, like peeling an onion. At his first thrust she felt herself die from the pain and an atrocious shock as if she were a calf being carved up. She was left breathless, drenched in icy sweat, but she appealed to her primal instincts to not feel inferior or let herself feel less than him, and they threw themselves into the inconceivable pleasure of brute force subjugated by tenderness. She never worried about finding out who he was, or even tried, until some three years after that brutal night, when she recognized him on television in a composite sketch of a sad vampire sought by police forces all over the Caribbean: a swindler who pimped helpless widows, the probable murderer of two of them.

4

***

ANA MAGDALENA BACH FOUND NEXT YEAR'S man on the ferry to the island. The clouds were threatening rain, the sea looked more like October, and it was not comfortable up on deck. A band started playing Caribbean music as soon as the boat set sail, and a group of German tourists danced without a break until they reached the island. At eleven in the morning she looked for a quiet place in the deserted dining room to concentrate on reading Ray Bradbury's *Martian Chronicles*. She had almost managed it when she was interrupted by a shout:

"This is my lucky day!"

Dr. Aquiles Coronado, a prestigious lawyer, a friend of hers since school, and godfather to her daughter, was approaching from the passageway with his laborious gait like that of a large primate, his arms open wide. Grabbing her around the waist, he lifted her off the floor and smothered her in kisses. His slightly theatrical congeniality triggered more suspicion than he deserved, but she knew his joy was sincere. She returned it just as cheerfully, and invited him to sit beside her.

"It's incredible," he said. "We never see each other anymore except at weddings and funerals."

In fact, they hadn't seen each other for three years, and the years showed so much that she was horrified by the idea he might be looking at her as astonished as she was at him. He still had his gladiator's impetuousness, but he had pebbly skin, a Renaissance double chin, and a few strands of yellowing hair blown up by the sea wind. When they first met back in high school he was already a specialist in seduction, the audacities of which went no further than a furtive six o'clock cinema visit. However, he had married advantageously, which brought him more money and more of a name than a whole lifetime devoted to the Civil Code.

His only failed conquest was Ana Magdalena Bach, who turned him down on his first attempt at the age of fifteen. Once they were both married and with children, he renewed his crude and slightly insolent offensive to try to take her to bed without any sentimental pretense. She subjected him to the deadly technique of not taking him seriously, but he redoubled his efforts, filling her house with flowers and sending her two ardent letters that actually managed to move her. However, she held firm on not destroying a lovely lifelong friendship.

When they met again on the boat he was irreproachable, and nobody was as well-mannered as he was when he put his mind to it. They said goodbye on the dock, as he barely had time to do what he had to do and return on the four o'clock ferry. She took a breath. She had dreamt of that next August 16, hour by hour, and the exercise left her in no doubt: it was absurd to wait a whole year to put the rest of her life at the mercy of one night's chance. She established that her first adventure had been a fortunate coincidence set within reach, but she had chosen it, while in the second she had been chosen. The first had been spoiled by the poor taste of the twenty dollars, but that man was worth the night. The second, however, had been the deflagration of a supernatural pleasure that left her threshed and burning and in need of three days of compresses and sitz baths.

As for the hotels, her usual had been the best, more manageable and more like her, but with the risk of being known there. The second year's had a repressive modernity that ended up in medieval moralism. After all, the error of dressing for the night in such a pretentious hotel could only increase the risk that a casual lover might leave not a twenty-dollar bill but a hundred. So the third time she decided to be herself, dress her normal way, and preserve her freedom to choose for herself and not leave it to chance. She remembered with a certain indulgence the first man and his lack of tact. She felt that the wounds were beginning to heal. She deeply desired to meet him and take him to bed, this time without fear or haste, and with the creative confidence of two longtime lovers.

With the help of a different taxi driver she chose a hotel with rustic cabins in an almond grove, with a big courtyard dance floor and tables for meals encircling it, and a poster announcing in huge letters a special appearance by Celia Cruz, the great Cuban singer. The cabin they assigned her seemed private and cool, the bed comfortable and wide enough even for three, and its placement among the trees could not be better. The fluttering in her chest became unbearable at the mere idea of having the love of her life until dawn.

It was still drizzling in the cemetery. She noticed they had cleared the weeds off the graves, leveled the paths, and removed the remains of old coffins and unclaimed bones. She gave her mother a detailed account of her husband's good year at the conservatory in spite of municipal financial troubles, her son's progress in the orchestra, and her failure to prevent her daughter from joining the convent.

Back at the hotel she saw a lovely embroidered huipil from Oaxaca in a tourist shop and thought it the most appropriate thing she could wear that night. She felt in absolute command of herself. She read the third story in *The Martian Chronicles* without being surprised, then called her husband, and they teased each other with affectionate jokes. She took a shower and admired herself in the mirror: as beautiful and free as the Aztec queen the huipil evoked, except for her patent leather shoes. She thought going barefoot would be appropriate for her evening's outfit, but she didn't dare. So she went to the dance floor with that fleeting frustration, yet with the certainty of anticipating fate.

The almond trees looked like they were decorated for Christmas with garlands of colored lights, and the patio was cheerful with young people of every stripe, blond girls with their black boyfriends, and resigned old married couples. She was sitting at a table apart from the rest, her antennae alert, when someone came up behind her and covered her eyes with his hands. She was in high spirits and touched them, recognizing a solid watch on the left wrist and a wedding ring on one finger, but did not hazard a name.

"I give up," she said.

It was Aquiles Coronado. He'd had to postpone his return until the next day, and it didn't seem fair for them each to be dining on their own when they were both alone on the island. He didn't know which hotel she was at, but her husband told him by phone, delighted to hear they'd have dinner together.

"I haven't had a minute's peace since we said goodbye, but here I am," he concluded happily. "The night is ours."

She felt the world sink beneath her feet, but kept her calm.

"On the boat you were impeccably behaved," she said with calculated charm. "I see age has brought you good sense."

"I'm afraid so," he said, "but don't imagine I'm happy about it."

She did not want champagne. She said she had a headache from the lunch on the ferry, and felt an icy nausea rising in her throat. He ordered a double whisky on the rocks. She made do with an aspirin, which she took as if it were poison.

The show began with a trio who specialized in songs by Los Panchos. Nobody paid much attention and Aquiles Coronado even less. He unburdened himself of a passion that had been building inside him since adolescence. Now, when he made love to his wife in the darkness, he could only think of Ana Magdalena Bach. She began to play for time so he would drink. She knew that one whisky after another would sweep him over the edge and she allowed him to carry on toward his own downfall. He knew that she would never oblige him out of pity, but still he begged her for one minute in bed, just one minute, to kiss her, even fully dressed. Not really knowing what to say, she said:

"Between godparents it's a mortal sin."

"I'm serious," he said, wounded by her teasing, and banged on the table. "Damn it!"

She dared to look him in the eyes and saw what she had heard in his voice: his face was streaming with tears. Then she stood up from the table without a word, walked back to her room, and threw herself on the bed to cry with rage.

When she recovered her mood it was after midnight. Her head hurt, but the loss of her night hurt more. She fixed herself up a little and went back ready to rescue it. She drank a gin and soda on a barstool in front of the garden abandoned by the early-rising tourists. Along came a drag queen with cartoonish muscles and gold bracelets and chains, golden hair, and skin reddened by suntan lotion. They sat at the bar drinking something phosphorescent. She wondered if she might be capable of flirting with the bartender, who was young and well-built, and decided she would not. She went so far as to wonder if she might be capable of walking the streets, stopping cars until she found someone who would do her her August favor, and the response was the same: no. Missing the night meant missing a year, but it was three in the morning and there was no alternative: it was lost.

Relations with her husband had undergone notable variations in those three years, and she interpreted them according to her state of mind when she returned from the island. The twenty-dollar man, whose memory embittered her, had opened her eyes to the reality of her marriage, sustained thus far by a conventional happiness that avoided disagreements in order not to stumble over them, the way people hide dirt under the rug. Never had they been happier than they were then. They understood each other without speaking, laughed their heads off at their own mischief, and made such reckless love they seemed like teenagers.

Their daughter's fate was resolved easily and without haste. They saw her off with an intimate soirée, and invited the jazz musician with his new girlfriend. He and Doménico improvised a very personal rendition of Béla Bartók's *Contrasts* for piano and saxophone, and they all became old friends at first sight.

They surrendered her to the Discalced Carmelites at an ordinary convent mass. Ana Magdalena and her husband dressed for a funeral, but Micaela arrived an hour late having not slept a wink, in her mother's huipil, the tennis shoes she always wore, a suitcase with her toiletries, and a Van Morrison album she'd been given at the last minute. An almost adolescent priest, with angry skin and one arm in a cast, devoted a festive sermon to her with one final opportunity to withdraw if she was unsure of her vocation. Ana Magdalena would have liked to pay her daughter the tribute of a farewell tear but could not manage it in such a conventional atmosphere.

Life had changed after the third trip. When

she came home, Ana Magdalena had the impression that her husband was starting to wonder about her nights on the island. For the first time, he wanted to know who she had seen. She could have told him about the whole incident with Aquiles Coronado, because her husband knew about those doddering sieges over the years, but she stopped herself in time. She didn't want to give him another reason to keep thinking about her nights on the island.

Their lovemaking had become different. Once provocative and naughty in bed, Doménico lost his appetite and seemed perturbed. Ana Magdalena did not attribute this to his age and instead concluded he must harbor some suspicion about her nights away. More reasoned reflection, however, turned the situation upside down. Then it was she who began to think her husband was incurring some secret fatigue away from home.

Ana Magdalena had adapted to him, become like him, and he knew her so well that they ended up being one and the same. Since before they were married she had been warned about her boyfriend's ways—his powers of seduction and devastating flirtatiousness, especially with his music students. She did not listen to rumors or allow herself to doubt him. However, when they became engaged she could not resist the temptation to ask. He denied it all. He told her in jest that he was a virgin, but he was so convincing that she married him under the illusion that it was true. Nothing bothered her until shortly before her daughter was born, when a friend from school she hadn't seen for years asked her at a public pool how she had managed to get her husband to break up with his girlfriend from adolescence. She cut this friend off, and not only erased her from her life but increased the distance she always kept even from her best friends.

Her reasons back then to trust her husband seemed categorical. In spite of being less than two months away from giving birth, neither the frequency nor the ardor of their lovemaking had diminished. So it was a biological impossibility that he would still have energy for another bed after having sated her. However, since the rumor persisted, she put him on the spot:

"Anything I find out about you is your fault."

There were no more incidents until after the third trip, when she soothed the sting of her own conscience with the suspicion that he was deceiving her. The signs were clear. Doménico stayed out until long past his official hours at the conservatory, when he arrived home he went straight to the bathroom to cover up any unfamiliar smells with his usual aftershave, and he gave overly precise explanations of where he had been, what he had done, and with whom, even though no one had asked. One night after a gala event where her husband had been unusually successful she decided to intercept him. He was reading the score to *Così fan tutte* in bed. She had just finished reading *The Ministry of Fear*, which she had started on the island; she switched off the light on her side and turned to face the wall without saying anything. Amused, he said: "Good night, señora." She realized she had neglected the ritual and rushed to make amends. "Oh, sorry, my love," she said, and gave him a routine goodnight kiss. He hummed very softly so he wouldn't keep her awake. All of a sudden, with her back still turned to him, she said: "For once in your life, Doménico, tell me the truth." He knew that his first name from her mouth was a sign of a storm, yet he persisted with his habitual serenity: "What is it?" She was no less calm:

"How many times have you been unfaithful to me?"

"Unfaithful, never," he said. "But if what you want to know is whether I've gone to bed with anyone else, years ago you warned me that you didn't want to know."

Moreover: when they got married she had told him she didn't care if he slept with another woman, as long as it wasn't always the same woman, or if it was just once. But at the hour of truth she reneged.

"Those are things a person goes around saying," she said, "and should not be taken literally."

"If I tell you I haven't, I'm sure you won't believe me," he said. "And if I tell you I have, you won't be able to bear it. What should we do?"

She knew no man would concoct such a roundabout way to say no, and forged ahead: "Who was the lucky lady?" He said naturally: "Someone in New York." She began to raise her voice: "But who?" "She was Chinese," he said. She felt her heart close up like a fist and regretted having provoked that futile pain, but even so she stubbornly insisted on knowing everything. For him, instead, the worst was over and he told her everything with a calculated reluctance.

It had happened some twelve years earlier, in the New York hotel where he stayed with his orchestra one weekend during a Wagner festival. The woman was the first violin in the Beijing Symphony Orchestra, with a room on the same floor. When he finished telling her, Ana Magdalena felt raw with pain. She wanted to kill them both, not with a merciful gunshot, but by carving them up bit by bit into transparent slices with a meat guillotine. But she exhaled through the wound to ask one more question that intrigued her:

"Did you pay her?"

He answered no, she was not a prostitute. She held her ground. "If she had been, how much would you have paid?" He thought it over seriously and didn't know how to answer. "Don't play dumb," she said, hoarse with rage. "Do you expect me to believe a man doesn't know how much a hotel hooker costs?" He was sincere. "Well, I don't actually know," he said, "especially not if she's from China." Then she besieged him with her unbearable anguish.

"Okay: if she had been friendly and good to you, and you wanted to give her a memento, how much would you have left between the pages of a book?"

"A book?" he said in surprise. "Whores don't read."

"Give me a break, damn it," she said, forcing herself not to lose her temper. "How much would you have left if you thought she was a whore and you didn't want to wake her up before you left?"

"I haven't got the slightest idea."

"Twenty dollars?"

He felt lost in the obscurity of the question. "I don't know," he said. "Maybe, given the cost of living twelve years ago, perhaps that would have been quite a lot." She closed her eyes to regulate her breathing to keep him from noticing her rage, and surprised herself by asking: "Did she have you horizontal?" He couldn't help but laugh, and she did too. But she stopped short and had to close her eyes to hold back tears.

"I'm laughing," she said with her hand on her chest, "but I hope you never have to feel what I'm feeling here inside. It's death."

He tried to ward off the bad moment by improvising a tune. She tried to go to sleep but could not. Finally she vented in a loud voice so he would hear her, even if he were asleep.

"Damn it," she said. "All men are the same shit."

He had to swallow his rage. He would have given anything to crush her with a lethal reply, but life had taught him that when a woman has the last word, any others are futile. So they did not speak of it again, neither then nor ever after.

5

———

THE NEXT AUGUST 16 WAS NOW SET TO BE HER destiny. She found the island in disarray due to an international tourism convention, not a single hotel room available, the beaches covered in tents and trailers. After spending two hours looking for anywhere to sleep, she turned to her forgotten Hotel del Senador, renovated, clean, and more expensive, but without any of the staff from her earlier visits.

There was no one to appeal to for a room. More than that: a respectable-looking guest was protesting indignantly because his twice-confirmed reservation did not appear on the list. He had the phlegmatic calm of an honorable chancellor, a deliberate and gentle voice, and a shocking talent for chivalrous insults. The only employee at the reception desk was phoning around trying to find him a room in another hotel. Eager to share his fury, the guest turned to Ana Magdalena. "This island is in chaos," he said, and showed her the official proof of his confirmed reservation. She could not read it without her glasses, but understood his indignation. Finally the employee interrupted them with the triumphant news that there was one room available—only a two-star hotel, but it was clean and well situated. Ana Magdalena hurried to ask:

"There wouldn't be another for me, would there?"

The employee asked over the phone and there was not. Then the guest picked up his suitcase with his left hand and with the other took Ana Magdalena by the arm with an unusual familiarity that struck her as rather outrageous.

"Come with me," he said. "We'll go and see."

They went in a new car, and he drove along the very edge of the lagoon. He said he liked the Hotel del Senador. "I do, too, because of the lagoon," she said, "and now I see they've renovated." "Two years ago," he said. She realized he was an assiduous visitor to the island, and she told him that she too had been coming here for years, to place a bouquet of gladioli on her mother's grave.

"Gladioli?" he asked in surprise, as he hadn't known there were any on the island. "I thought you could only find them in Holland."

"Those are tulips," she clarified.

She explained that gladioli are not very common, but someone had brought them to the island and they had thrived, just along the coast and in some other interior villages. For her they were so important, she concluded, that if the day came when there weren't any she would arrange for someone to grow them.

It began to drizzle, but it didn't look set to last. He thought the opposite, because the weather in August always seemed erratic. He looked her up and down, with her simple clothes for the ferry crossing, and suggested she would need something more for the cemetery. But she reassured him: she was used to it.

Their route took them around the lagoon to the poorest edge of the village. The hotel was deplorable, undoubtedly a place for assignations where they didn't ask to see identification at reception. When he received the key, the guest clarified that they needed two rooms.

"Sorry," said the doorman, disconcerted. "Are you not together?"

"She is my wife," the guest said with his natural charm, "but we have the hygienic custom of sleeping separately."

She played along:

"The farther apart the better."

The doorman admitted that the bed in the room was not very wide, but he could bring up a cot. The guest was stumped, but she rescued him. "If you heard him snore you wouldn't suggest such a thing," she told the doorman. He excused himself, examined the keys hanging on the board while they celebrated their prank, and finally said he could sort out another room, on a different floor and without a view of the lagoon. They went up in the elevator without a bellboy—both suitcases were small. She got off on the second floor and he went on to the fourth. She was full of gratitude, pleased to have met such a kind man.

The room was small, like a cabin on a boat, but with a bed big enough for three, which seemed to be a distinguishing feature of the island. She opened the window to air the place out and only then did she realize how much she'd missed the flowers and the blue herons of the lagoon. It was still raining, but she was sure it would let up in time for her to get to the cemetery before six.

And so it did, although she wasted more than an hour looking for gladioli, which she finally found at a stall in front of the church. The taxi that took her to the cemetery could not drive up to the summit due to the terrible state of the cliff road. The driver would agree only to wait at a bend in the road until she got back. She suddenly realized that on the twenty-fifth of November she would turn fifty, the age she most feared, not much younger than her mother had been when she died. She looked as she had looked a few years earlier, waiting for the sky to clear, and wept as she had wept ever since she'd first brought a bouquet of flowers to the grave. But her weeping seemed to appease the sky's bad mood. It cleared up suddenly and she placed the flowers on the grave.

She went back to the hotel covered in mud and in a bad mood, and took it for granted that she had lost another year. It didn't seem possible that she could find a lover for the night, even if she flagged down cars on the promenade turned into a horrendous quagmire by the rain. Nothing had changed. The headless shower barely trickled, and as she lathered up under the scrawny stream she felt lonely—without even a benevolent man—and began to cry again. But she didn't give up: she would go out in any case and see what that ungainly night might provide. She hung up her clothes and put her book on the bedside table. It was Daniel Defoe's *A Journal of the Plague Year,* and she lay down to read until it was time to go to the bar. But everything seemed arranged on purpose to deny her pleasure. The paltry shower had made her feel even more miserable, and she shuddered with a burst of hatred against her husband so violent and cold that it startled her. She had just resigned herself, on this lousy night, to the sinister fate of sleeping alone, when the telephone rang.

"Hello," said a cheerful voice that she recognized immediately. "This is your friend from the fourth floor." And he added in a different tone: "I've been waiting for a response, even if only out of charity." And after a long pause he asked:

"Did you not receive the flowers?"

She did not understand. She was going to ask, when her gaze fell upon a bouquet of splendid gladioli placed carelessly on the chair by the dressing table. The man explained that he had found them by chance at the hotel where he was meeting clients and it seemed natural to send them for her mother's grave. She hadn't noticed when they'd been delivered, perhaps while she'd been at the cemetery, but they could just as well have been there before that. Out of nowhere, he asked her casually:

"Where are you having dinner?"

"I hadn't thought about it," she said.

"It doesn't matter," he said. "I'll wait for you downstairs to decide."

Another frustrated night, she thought, with another Aquiles? No.

"What a shame," she said. "I have a commitment this evening."

"Yes, a shame," he said, truly sorry.

"We'll have to do it another time," she said.

She fixed her face before the mirror. She had thought of going to the place where she'd been

on the miserable night with Aquiles Coronado,
but the rain intensified and the wind howled
across the lagoon. She suddenly shouted at herself: "God in heaven, how beastly of me!"

She ran to the phone and called the man in
the room on the fourth floor with a haste that
would later embarrass her.

"What a stroke of luck!" she said without
skipping a beat. "They've just canceled because
of the rain."

"The luck is mine, señora," he said.

She did not hesitate for an instant. And she
was not wrong: it was an unforgettable night.

Much less forgettable than Ana Magdalena
Bach could have imagined. She had taken more
time than was necessary to fix herself up, and
the man was waiting for her by the elevator
door, wearing a silk guayabera, linen trousers,
and white moccasins. She confirmed her first
impression: he was attractive, even more so
because he acted as if he did not know it. He
drove her to a restaurant outside of the touristy

hives, beneath giant illuminated almond trees and with an orchestra better for dreaming than for dancing. He walked in with great presence, was well received as a longstanding customer, and behaved as if that's what he was. His manners had become more refined with the splendor of the night. His whole being radiated a distinctive air through his fresh eau de cologne, and his conversation was free-flowing and pleasant. But she felt a little lost, for he seemed to be talking not so much to speak as to hide.

He surprised her with his lack of skill in choosing drinks. He waited for her to choose her usual gin, then ordered a whisky without specifying a brand, and didn't touch it all night. He did not smoke: his packet of Egyptian cigars rolled in gold paper was just to offer. He was not practiced in the art of fine dining, and allowed the waiter to decide for them. But the most surprising thing was that with all his limitations and mistakes he did not lose a whit of charm, not even when he came out with two or three jokes so silly and badly told that she couldn't understand them and had to laugh simply out of courtesy.

When the band started playing a danceable arrangement of Aaron Copland, he confessed that he hadn't noticed because he was tone deaf. He went along, though, when she asked him to dance. He didn't get the steps right, but she helped him so subtly that he thought he was figuring it out himself.

By the time dessert came, she was so bored she cursed herself for her weakness, even more so when a man walked past whom she would have chosen with her eyes closed. Her date was so decent that he didn't put a foot wrong except while dancing—he treated her well and she felt fine—but still, the night held no promise.

As soon as they finished their desserts he took her back to the hotel, driving in silence, their gazes absorbed by the sleeping sea beneath a fanciful moon. She did not interrupt it. It was ten past eleven and even the bar of their hotel would be closed. What made her most indignant was not having anything to reproach her date for. His only fault had been not trying to seduce her: not even a compliment on her radiant lioness eyes or her flowing conversation or her musical knowledge.

He parked in front of the hotel and accompanied her up in the elevator in absolute silence, then to the door of her room. She fumbled with the key and he took it from her, opened the door with his fingertips, walked in with neither invitation nor permission, making himself at home, and collapsed on the bed face up with a heartfelt sigh:

"This is the night of a lifetime!"

Ana Magdalena stood petrified, not knowing what to do, until he held out his hand in silence. She gave him hers and lay down beside him, bewildered by the beating of her heart. He then gave her an innocent kiss that shook her to her core, and kept kissing her while removing her clothes piece by piece with magical mastery, until they succumbed to an abyss of pleasure.

When Ana Magdalena woke up in the semi-

darkness of dawn she had lost all sense of herself. She didn't know where she was or who she
was with, until she saw the completely naked
man beside her, sleeping on his back with his
arms crossed over his chest and breathing like a
baby in a crib. She tenuously caressed his curls
and suntanned skin with one finger. He did not
have a young body, but it was well cared for, and
he enjoyed the caresses without opening his
eyes and with as much self-control as he had
shown in the night, until love made him unruly.

"Seriously now," he asked out of the blue:
"what's your name?"

She improvised.

"Perpetua."

"She was a poor saint who died under the
hoofs of a cow," he said immediately.

Surprised, she asked how he knew that.

"I'm a bishop," he said.

She shuddered with a deathly flash. She
went back over the dinner, his elaborate conversation, his conventional tastes, and couldn't
find anything to belie his answer. Furthermore:

it confirmed what she had thought during the course of the meal. He noticed her recoiling, opened his eyes and, intrigued, asked:

"What do you have against us?"

"Against whom?"

"Us bishops."

He burst out laughing radiantly at the effect of his own joke but soon understood that it was in bad taste and covered her body in long contrite kisses. Maybe as a penance he told her a version of his actual life story. He had worked at different jobs and did not have a fixed address, because his basic trade was selling maritime insurance for a company with headquarters in Curaçao, and he had to visit the island several times a year. At first his powers of persuasion were so strong that she felt overcome, but her conviction that it was already too late to be pleasured three times in one night prevailed.

"I'm going to miss the ferry," she said.

"That doesn't matter," he said. "We'll go together tomorrow."

He proposed a great day and many more in

the future, for he had to return to the island at least twice a year, and one of his trips could always be in August. She listened to him worried that he meant it, but she had the strength not to appear as easy a woman as he might think. She suddenly realized that she really was about to miss the ferry, so she leapt out of bed and said goodbye with a hurried kiss. But he grabbed her clenched fist.

"And so," he insisted: "until when?"

"Until never again," she said and concluded cheerfully: "It's God's will."

She ran into the bathroom and locked the door without listening to the list of promises he pursued her with as he finished dressing. She barely had time to turn off the shower when he knocked on the door to complete his farewell.

"I left you a souvenir in your book," he said.

She felt struck by a sinister omen. She didn't dare say thank you or ask what he had left, terrified of what he might reply, but as soon as she heard him leave she ran out naked, covered in soap, to examine the book on the bedside table.

What a relief! It was a visitor's card with all his contact details. She didn't tear it up, as she undoubtedly would have done with any other, but left it where it was until she could put it in a safe place.

6

IT WAS A TYPICAL WEDNESDAY IN AUGUST ON
the Caribbean, with a sleepy sea and a tenuous breeze for low-gliding gulls. Ana Magdalena
Bach rolled a deck chair over to the ferry railing
and opened her Daniel Defoe book to the page
marked by the visitor's card, but she could not
concentrate. The card itself, with its particu-
lars of the previous night's man, couldn't hold
her attention either: he had a Dutch name and
nationality, a commercial address with six telephone numbers, and a technical services business with headquarters in Curaçao. She read it

several times trying to imagine the phantom of her happy night in his real life. However, since her encounter with the first man, she had taken the precaution of never leaving the slightest trace that could stir any suspicion in her home. So she tore up the card into minuscule pieces and tossed them into the seagulls' complicit breeze.

It was a revealing return. From the moment she entered the house at five in the afternoon she discovered the extent to which she was starting to feel like a stranger in her own family. Her daughter had assimilated into convent life without losing herself, and she gradually became a less frequent presence at her parents' table. Her son barely had any free time between his fleeting love affairs and his artistic commitments all over the world. Her husband, being both a workaholic and an inveterate flirt, had ended up only a casual guest in her bed lately. For her, however, the strangest paradox was discovering that she was losing the illusion of the island: among the men she'd tried by chance on her limited nights, there was no sure option. Still, her greatest anxiety was not her suspicion about her husband's fidelity but her dread that he had a hunch about what she did on those few nights she spent on the island. For that very reason she avoided making comments about her annual trips so it would not occur to him to go with her, or so as not to arouse any male doubts, which are not easily provoked but almost always infallible.

There were simple years with no time or opportunity for betrayals or jealousy. She kept rigorous track of her cycles to allow for frequent lovemaking. They didn't leave the city without her making sure she had condoms in her purse for unexpected occasions. This time, however, she felt a stab in her heart when he arrived home covered in such outrageous clues that they incited sudden suspicions not only of that year but of all the years that had gone before. She watched him, she examined the seams of his pockets, and for the first time she started sniffing the clothes he'd worn and left lying on the bed. Starting in May, however, a dream of the man from the year before shook her to her soul. The anxiety took her breath away. She cursed once again the moment she'd torn up his card, and now felt incapable of happiness without him, even if only on the island. Her restlessness was so obvious that her husband said without beating around the bush: "Something's up with you."

Her terror aggravated her insomnia until dawn, for she herself did not seem aware of how much she'd started to change since her first trips. She had never considered the risk of running into someone she knew from the island, until the dreadful night when her daughter's godfather, Aquiles Coronado, had too much to drink at a wedding and dropped a few unfunny veiled comments that more than four of their table companions could have deciphered without much effort. On the other hand, one afternoon when she was having lunch with three friends in the city's most prestigious restaurant, she thought she recognized one of the two men who were deep in quiet conversation at an isolated table. They had a bottle of brandy, their glasses were half full, and they seemed alone in a separate life. But the one in her line of vision had an impeccable white linen suit that fit him well, ash-colored hair, and a romantic pointed moustache. From the first glance she had the impression she knew him. But however much she strained she could not remember who he was or where she had seen him before. More than once she lost the thread of the animated chat with her friends, until one of them couldn't contain her curiosity and asked her what was worrying her at the next table.

"The one with the Turkish moustache," she whispered. "I don't know why but he reminds me of someone."

They all looked stealthily. "Well, he's not bad," said one of them without interest, and they resumed their chitchat. But Ana Magdalena was still so unsettled that she had trouble falling asleep that night and woke up at three in the morning with her heart bristling. Her husband woke up, too, but she managed to catch her breath and told him about a fake nightmare that resembled many other real and terrifying ones that used to wake her when they were newlyweds. For the first time she wondered why she didn't dare do in the city what she did on the island. Here, she had the whole year available with daily and much more manageable opportunities. At least five of her friends had conducted furtive love affairs for as long as they'd had the energy and had maintained stable marriages at the same time. Nevertheless, she could not imagine any situation in the city as exciting or suitable as the island, which she could understand only as a posthumous scheme of her mother's.

For several weeks she could not resist the temptation of encountering this man who would not let her live in peace. She returned to the restaurant at the busiest times, never missing a chance to drag a couple of floating friends along to avoid any misunderstandings about her solitary wanderings. She grew accustomed to confronting any men she found along the way, longing to or fearful of finding her own. However, she needed no help at all when the man's identity finally burst into her memory like a blinding explosion. It was the very man who on that first night of love on the island had committed the disgraceful act of leaving that twenty-dollar bill between the pages of her book. Only then did she realize that maybe she hadn't been able to recognize him because of the musketeer's moustache, which he did not have at the time. She became a regular customer at the restaurant where she had seen him, always with a twenty-dollar bill ready to throw in his face, yet she was increasingly less clear about what her attitude should be: the more she delved into her rage, the less the bad memory mattered.

However, when August arrived she felt more than strong enough to carry on being herself. The ferry crossing seemed endless as always, the same island that she'd so often dreamt of seemed noisier and even poorer, and the taxi that took her to the same hotel as the previous year's almost went over the edge of a narrow mountain pass. The room where she had been happy was available, and the same doorman immediately remembered the guest who had accompanied her but could not find any trace of him in the files. She made an anxious tour of other places where they'd been together and found all sorts of aimless men on their own who would have sufficed to alleviate her night, but none looked good enough to replace the one she was longing for. So she checked into the same room of the same hotel as the year before and went straight to the cemetery for fear the rain would get there before her.

With scarcely bearable anxiety she retraced her every step to fulfill quickly and painlessly her annual routine up to her encounter with her mother. The same florist as always, older every year, at first glance confused her with someone else. She made a bouquet of gladioli as splendid as ever, but with enormous reluctance and at almost twice the price.

In front of her mother's grave Ana Magdalena was shocked to find an unusual heap of flowers, rotted from the rains. Unable to imagine who had put them there, she asked the caretaker without the slightest suspicion, and he answered with the same innocence:

"The gentleman who always does."

Her bewilderment grew when the caretaker explained that he had no idea who the unknown visitor could be. The gentleman might arrive any day of the year and leave the grave completely covered in those splendid flowers, the likes of which were never seen in a cemetery for poor people. So many and so expensive that it pained the caretaker to remove them if even the slightest trace of their natural splendor remained. He described the gentleman: about seventy well-lived years, with snowy hair, a senator's moustache, and a cane that turned into an umbrella so he could remain absorbed in front of the grave while it rained. The caretaker never asked him anything and never told anyone about the wealth of the gentleman's flowers or the size of his tips. He hadn't mentioned it to her on her previous visits because he was sure that the gentleman with the magic umbrella must be a member of the family.

She swallowed her concern and gave the caretaker a good tip, overwhelmed by the blazing revelation that might explain all at once the secret of her mother's frequent trips to the island, camouflaged as some business of hers that no one had a clear idea of and perhaps did not exist.

Ana Magdalena Bach left the cemetery a different woman. She was trembling, and the driver had to help her into the taxi because she could not control her body's shaking. Only then did she understand her mother's determination to be buried there, on an island she visited three or four times a year, when she learned she was dying of a terrible illness in a foreign land. Only then did the daughter glimpse the reason her mother had taken those trips the six years before she died. She considered that her mother's reason—her mother's passion—might be the same as hers, and surprised herself with the analogy. She did not feel sad but rather encouraged by the realization that the miracle of her life was to have continued that of her dead mother.

Overwhelmed by the emotions of that afternoon, Ana Magdalena wandered aimlessly through poor neighborhoods and somehow found herself in the tent of an itinerant magician who could guess with his saxophone whatever popular melody someone in the audience was remembering in silence. Ana Magdalena would never have dared take part, but that night she asked in jest where the man of her dreams was. The magician answered with an accurate imprecision:

"Neither as near as you wish nor as far as you believe."

She returned to her hotel without having fixed herself up and with her mood dragging on the floor. The outdoor terrace was heaving with young people dancing, their hearts on their sleeves, to the music of a young band, and she could not resist the temptation to share the joy of a cheerful generation. There was not a single free table, but the waiter recognized her from previous years and brought her one as fast as he could.

After the first dance session, another, more ambitious band began to play Debussy's "Clair de lune" in a bolero arrangement, and a gorgeous young woman sang it with love. Moved, Ana Magdalena ordered her usual gin with ice and soda, the only alcohol she still allowed herself now that she was fifty.

The only thing that seemed at odds with the mood of the night was the couple at the next table: he, young and attractive, and she perhaps older, but dazzling and haughty. They were obviously in a silent fight, exchanging ferocious reproaches that missed their mark in the uproar of the fiesta. In the breaks between songs they would pause intensely so they wouldn't be overheard by nearby tables, but then renewed their fight with more momentum during the next piece. An episode so common in that anonymous world that Ana Magdalena didn't take any interest, even as a sideshow. But her heart skipped a beat when the woman broke her glass on the table with theatrical solemnity and walked across the dance floor in a straight line without looking at anyone, proud and beautiful, through the crowd of happy couples who moved out of her way. Ana Magdalena understood that the fight had ended, but she had the discretion not to look at the man, who stayed where he was, undaunted.

When the official band finished their set, another, more ambitious band started with the nostalgic "Siboney," and Ana Magdalena let herself get swept up by the magic of the music mixed with gin. All of a sudden, in a break between songs her eyes chanced to meet those of the man abandoned at the next table. She did not look away. He returned her gaze with

a slight nod, and she felt she was reliving a distant episode from her adolescence. She was
bewildered by a strange shiver—as if it were the
first time—and the embers of the gin instilled
in her a courage not her own to take it all the
way. He got there first.

"That man is a swine," he said.

She was surprised:

"What man?"

"The one who left you waiting," he said.

It wrenched her heart to think that he
was talking to her as if he could see her from
within, and she answered him informally and
sarcastically.

"From what I've just seen you're the one
who got the door slammed in your face."

He realized she was referring to the incident
that had just left him on his own. "We always
end up with a tantrum like that, but it doesn't
last long," he said. And he went on to his final
point: "You, however, have no reason to be
alone". She wrapped him in a bitter look.

"At my age," she said, "all women are alone."

"In that case," he said with renewed energy, "this is my lucky night."

He stood up, glass in hand, and sat down at her table without further ado, and she felt so sad and lonely that she didn't stop him. He ordered her a glass of her favorite gin, and for a moment she forgot her woes and went back to being the same as she was on other nights of solitude. She once again cursed the hour she'd torn up her last man's card, and did not feel capable of happiness without him that night, even if only for an hour. So she danced purely out of apathy, but the man danced well and made her feel better.

When they returned to the table after a set of waltzes, she realized she didn't have the key to her room and looked for it in her purse and under the table. He pulled it out of his pocket with a parody of a conjurer's flourish and sang out her room number as if he were a roulette caller:

"The lucky number: three hundred and thirty-three!"

People at neighboring tables turned to look at them. She could not stand the vulgarity of the joke and held out her hand with a severe expression. He realized his mistake and returned her key. She took it in silence and left the table.

"At least allow me to accompany you," he begged, following her blindly. "Nobody should be alone on a night like this."

He jumped up from his chair, perhaps to say goodnight or perhaps to accompany her. Maybe he himself did not know, but she thought she could guess his intention. "Don't bother," she told him. He seemed overwhelmed.

"Not to worry," she insisted. "My son would have pulled that same stunt when he was seven."

She left decisively, but she had not even reached the elevator when she started to wonder if she hadn't just snubbed happiness on the night she most needed it. She fell asleep with the lights on, arguing with herself about whether she should go to sleep or back down to the bar to confront her destiny. A recurring nightmare of her darkest hours had begun to perturb her when a few furtive knocks on the door woke her up. The lights were still on, and she was face down on the bed, on top of the bedclothes without realizing it. She stayed like that, biting the tear-soaked pillow so she wouldn't have to ask who it was, until the person who was knocking stopped. Then she made herself comfortable in the bed, without changing her clothes or switching off the lights, and cried herself to sleep furious with herself for the disgrace of being a woman in a man's world.

She had not slept more than four hours when a call from reception woke her so she wouldn't miss the eight o'clock ferry. She got up determined to take the plunge she hadn't known how to take during her bad island nights. But she had to wait two hours for the cemetery caretaker so he could inform her what forms she needed to fill out to have her mother's remains exhumed. Only when she was sure it would happen, past noon by then, did she phone her husband and lie to him that she'd missed the ferry but would definitely be on the afternoon one.

The caretaker and a hired gravedigger dis-
interred the coffin and opened it with no compassion but with the artistry of a fairground
magician. Ana Magdalena saw herself in the
open casket as if she were looking in a full-
length mirror, with a frozen smile and arms
folded on her chest. She looked identical and
the same age as on that day, with the veil and
tiara in which she'd been married, the red emerald diadem and her wedding rings, just as her
mother had stipulated with her last sigh. Not
only did she see her as she had been in life,
with the same inconsolable sadness, but she
felt seen by her from death, loved and wept for,
until the body disintegrated into dust and all
that was left was the decayed skeleton, which
the gravediggers brushed off with a broom and
swept pitilessly into a sack.

Two hours later, Ana Magdalena took a final
compassionate glance at her own past and
said goodbye forever to her one-night strang-
ers and to the hours and hours of uncertainties
that remained of herself scattered around the

island. The sea was an oasis of gold under the afternoon sun. At six, when her husband saw her walk into the house dragging the bag of bones matter-of-factly, he couldn't help but be surprised. "It's what's left of my mother," she told him, anticipating his fright.

"Don't be scared," she said. "She understands. She's the only one who could. What's more, I think she'd already understood when she decided to be buried on that island."

EDITOR'S NOTE
TO THE SPANISH EDITION

On March 18, 1999, Gabriel García Márquez's readers received the happy news that the Colombian Nobel laureate was working on a new book comprised of five autonomous tales with the same protagonist: Ana Magdalena Bach. The journalist Rosa Mora published the exclusive in the Spanish newspaper *El País* three days later alongside the first story of the book, "En agosto nos vemos" (Edith Grossman's translation, "Meeting in August," would appear in *The New Yorker* later that same year). García Márquez had read it aloud a few days earlier in the Casa de América in Madrid, where he was participating together with another Nobel laureate, José Saramago, in a forum on the strength of Ibero-American creativity. Instead of giving a speech, he surprised his audience by reading an early version of the first chapter of the novel the reader now has in hand. Rosa Mora added: "'En agosto nos vemos' will form part of a book that will include another three 150-page novellas, that Gabo has already practically written, and will probably include a fourth, because, as he explains, he's had another idea he's drawn to. The common denominator of the book is that they will be love stories between older people."

A few years later fortune crossed my destiny with that of García Márquez, one of my touchstone authors since adolescence. My impassioned reading of his work, along with that of Juan Rulfo, Jorge Luis Borges, and Julio Cortázar, had led me to cross the Atlantic to pursue a doctorate in Latin American literature at the University of Texas at Austin. In August of 2001, I was back in Barcelona working as an editor at

Random House Mondadori when Carmen Balcells summoned me to a meeting at her agency,
which was almost empty in the summer. She
wanted me to speak on the phone with García Márquez, who needed a trusted editor for
his memoirs. His usual editor, my dear friend
Claudio López de Lamadrid, was on vacation.
Thus began my shoulder-to-shoulder work with
the Colombian writer on the final version of
Vivir para contarla (*Living to Tell the Tale*), revising a manuscript that arrived by drip feed into
my email inbox or by fax and that I returned
with my annotations, which mostly consisted
of fact-checking. He was especially grateful for
the information that Kafka's *Metamorphosis,*
the reading of which had changed his narrative universe, had not actually been translated
into Spanish by Borges, even though the Argen-
tinian edition he'd read proclaimed on the
cover that it had been. Although he was in Los
Angeles recovering from an illness, the long-
distance editorial work allowed me to witness
the writer's craftsmanship, from the rewriting

of the chapter devoted to the "Bogotazo" to the brilliant change of a single letter in the Spanish title to avoid a conflict with another author. Even though an unexpected chance allowed me to meet him personally along with his wife, Mercedes Barcha, in a Barcelona restaurant, we did not renew our author-editor relationship until 2008.

In May 2003, after a long stay in Los Angeles, Gabriel García Márquez and Mercedes Barcha returned to their house in Mexico, where they were met by a new personal secretary they had just hired, Mónica Alonso. Her account was crucial in reconstructing the chronology of the creation of *Until August*. According to Mónica Alonso, on June 9, 2002, the writer finished revising the final galleys of his memoir, with the editor Antonio Bolívar's assistance. After clearing his desk of various versions and notes for the submitted book, he received the news that his mother had died that very day. With that enigmatic coincidence, the circle that had begun with the opening of his memoir—"My mother asked me to go with her to sell the house"—was now closed. The writer found himself without an imminent project when, going through the drawers in his study, Mónica found a folder that contained two manuscripts: one called "Ella" and the other "En agosto nos vemos." Between August 2002 until July 2003 García Márquez worked intensely on "Ella," the title of which he would change to *Memoria de mis putas tristes / Memories of My Melancholy Whores* when it was published in 2004/5. This would be the last work of fiction published in his lifetime.

But the publication in May 2003 of another fragment of *Until August* would seem to be a public declaration that García Márquez was still moving forward with his last narrative project. The third chapter of *Until August* came out as an unpublished short story, with the title "The Night of the Eclipse," in the Colombian magazine *Cambio* on May 19, 2003 and a few days later in *El País*. According to Mónica Alonso, starting in July 2003 the writer began to work intensely again on the manuscript of the novel.

That's how, from then until the end of 2004, he accumulated five successively numbered versions, apart from a few early first drafts and a version that he had brought back from Los Angeles. All these dated versions are among the writer's papers in safekeeping at the Harry Ransom Center of the University of Texas at Austin.

After reaching the fifth version he stopped work on the novel and sent a copy to Carmen Balcells. "Sometimes books need to be left to rest," he confided to Mónica Alonso. An important event awaited him, the celebration of the fortieth anniversary of the publication of *Cien años de soledad*, with a commemorative edition by the Real Academia Española, and the preparations were going to keep him busy. His participation in the opening session of the congress, on March 26, 2007, in Cartagena, would be one of his last big public events.

In March 2008, now settled in Mexico as editorial director of Random House Mondadori, I resumed my relationship as his editor. Carmen Balcells put me in charge of working with García Márquez on a book collecting his public speeches, which would be published two years later under the title *Yo no vengo a decir un discurso / I'm Not Here to Give a Speech*. Frequent visits to his study, at least once a month, turned into a long conversation about books, authors, and the subjects covered in the speeches themselves.

In the summer of 2010 Carmen Balcells informed me in Barcelona that García Márquez had an unpublished novel that he couldn't find an ending for, and asked me to encourage him to finish it. She told me it was about a mature married woman who visits the island where her mother is buried and finds the love of her life. Upon my return to Mexico the first thing I did was ask Gabo about the novel and repeat his agent's words. Gabo was amused and confessed that it wasn't the love of her life that his protagonist finds but a different lover on each visit. And to prove that he did indeed have an ending, he asked Mónica for the latest version, in one of the German Leuchtturm binders he always used for his manuscripts, and he read me the last paragraph that closed the story in a dazzling way. He was very protective of his work in progress, but a few months later he allowed me to read three chapters out loud to him. I remember the impression I was left with: absolute mastery of an original theme he had not tackled previously in his work, and the desire that one day his readers could share it.

His memory did not allow him to fit together all the pieces and corrections of his last version, but the revision of the text was for a time the best way to occupy his days in his study, doing what he most enjoyed: suggesting an adjective to change here, or a detail there. Version 5, dated July 5, 2004, was clearly his favorite, and on its first page he wrote "Grand final OK. Info about her CH 2. NB: probable Final ch / Is it the best?" He decided with Mónica to overturn some of the suggestions annotated on previous versions. Mónica also kept a digital version which contained all the fragments of other options or scenes the author had previously considered. Those two documents are the basis of this edition.

The relationship between an author and an editor is a pact of trust based on respect. The privilege of working with Gabriel García Márquez is a constant exercise in humility that, in my case, was laid down in his own words when Carmen passed me the telephone for our first conversation: "I want you to be as critical as possible, since once I decide it's finished I don't revise anything." My work on this edition has been that of a restorer facing a great master's canvas. Starting from the digital document kept by Mónica Alonso, and comparing it to version 5, where he consolidated small corrections from other versions. I have checked each of his annotations, handwritten or dictated to Mónica, each modified or cut word or sentence, each option in the margin, to decide whether to incorporate it into this final version. An editor's task does not consist of changing a book but of making what is already on the page stronger, and that has been the essence of my work. That includes, among other things, checking and correcting facts, from the names of musicians or authors mentioned to the coherence of the age of the protagonist as he had planned in his marginal notes.

I hope that readers of *Until August* share the same respect and astonishment that I have felt the dozens of times I have read this text, readings during which I've sensed the presence of Gabo over my shoulder, as in the photo Mónica took of us together one day when we were checking the proofs of his book of speeches.

My gratitude to Rodrigo and Gonzalo García Barcha for the trust they placed in me that August day when they called to tell me they'd decided that *Until August* should be published and that I would be the editor. This was a daunting responsibility, but their encouragement and trust throughout the process has been the greatest recompense for the editorial assignment of a lifetime. The memory of Mercedes Barcha, who decided to open the doors of her house to me as well as the study, has been ever present in these months. Mónica Alonso's fidelity and commitment to the writer have been essential to getting the text into our hands and I thank her for the time she has devoted to reconstructing the history of its writing. We are also all in debt to the team at the Harry Ransom Center at the University of Texas at Austin, where the writer's archives are housed, for their work of digitally reproducing the manuscripts of the novel, essential to piloting this edition into harbor: Stephen Enniss, Jim Kuhn, Vivie Behrens, Cassandra Chen, Elizabeth Garver, and Alejandra Martínez. I thank my friend the great editor Gary Fisketjon for a conversation that helped me overcome a bout of editor's block. His experience has served as a guide, as has that of our much-missed editor in chief, Sonny Mehta, who would have loved to publish this book. Very special thanks to my wife, Elizabeth, and our children, Nicholas and Valerie, for their support during my long spells shut up in the attic with this novel. Finally, my most profound gratitude to Gabo, for his humanity, simplicity, and the affection he always served up to anyone who approached thinking he was a god, to demonstrate with his smile that he was a man. His memory over these months has been the greatest incentive to getting here.

—*Cristóbal Pera*
February 2023

THE ORIGINAL MANUSCRIPT
FOUR FACSIMILE PAGES

Here are four sample facsimile pages from the file labeled "Version 5" of *En agosto nos vemos*. These files were sorted and classified by García Márquez's secretary, Mónica Alonso, who also maintained a Word document from which the different versions gradually emerged. In his last years, when he could no longer work on his overall vision of the novel, García Márquez made small corrections, suggestions, and changes to other versions, that were consolidated in this version, on which he wrote "Gran OK final."

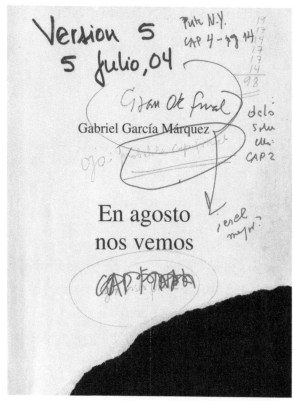

The title page of Version 5
In his final years, García Márquez merged his annotations from previous versions onto this version. Even though on this first page it says "Gran OK final," the version still contains fragments that were corrected in the Word document kept by his secretary, Mónica Alonso.

V. Cap 1   3

↓ 8̊ 3

vísperas de la tercera edad. Se estiró las mejillas hacia atrás
con los cantos de las manos para acordarse de cómo había
sido de joven. Pasó por alto las arrugas del cuello, que no
tenían remedio, y se revisó los dientes perfectos y recién
cepillados después del almuerzo en el transbordador. Se frotó
con el pomo del desodorante las axilas bien afeitadas y se
puso la camisa de algodón fresco con las inciales AMB
bordadas a mano en el bolsillo. Se cepilló el cabello indio,
largo hasta los hombros, y se amarró la cola de caballo con la
pañoleta de pájaros. Para terminar se suavizó los labios con el
lápiz labial de vaselina simple, se humedeció los índices en la
lengua para alisarse las cejas encontradas, se dio un toque de
Maderas de Oriente detrás de cada oreja, y se enfrentó por fin
al espejo con su rostro de madre otoñal. La piel sin un rastro
de cosméticos tenía el color y la textura de la melaza, y los
ojos de topacio eran hermosos con oscuros párpados
portugueses. Se trituró a fondo, se juzgó sin piedad, y se
encontró casi tan bien como se sentía. Sólo cuando se puso el
anillo y el reloj se dio cuenta de su retraso: faltaban seis para
las cuatro, Pero se concedió un minuto de nostalgia para
contemplar las garzas que planeaban inmóviles en el vapor
ardiente de la laguna. Los nubarrones negros del lado del

Page 3 of Version 5
On this page we can see some corrections that García Márquez
added to his text in later readings. The reference to the protagonist
being on the verge of "la tercera edad" or "the third age" appears
with a question mark above it and disappears from the final edition,
as Ana Magdalena Bach is forty-six years old. The digital version contains other small variations.

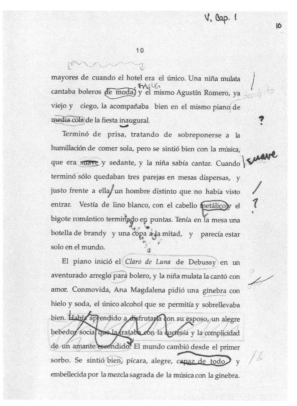

Page 10 of Version 5

The reference to the "bigote romántico terminado en puntas" or "romantic pointed moustache" worn by the man from chapter one disappears from the final edition. In chapter six, Ana Magdalena Bach runs into the same man in the city, but it takes her a while to identify him because he'd been clean-shaven when she'd met him: "Only then did she realize that maybe she hadn't been able to recognize him because of the musketeer's moustache, which he did not have at the time."

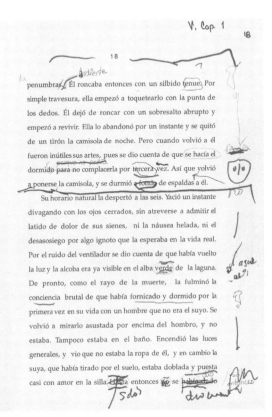

Page 18 of Version 5

On this page, as on many others, we can see corrections in the hand-writing of García Márquez's secretary, Mónica Alonso. Here Mónica adds the adjective "ardiente." It was usual in some sessions for her to read the text aloud, and García Márquez would ask her to add a note to change something here or there. At the same time, other changes would be put into the digital version, such as the doubt about the adjective "tenue," which eventually became "continuo."

A NOTE ON THE TYPE

The text of this book was set in Freight Text Pro Book, designed by Joshua Darden (b. 1979) and published by GarageFonts in 2005. It was inspired by the "Dutch- taste" school of typeface design and is considered a transitional-style typeface. Legible, stylish, and sturdy, Freight Text was designed to be highly versatile, belonging to a wide-ranging "superfamily" of fonts, including many versions and weights.

Composed by North Market Street Graphics,
Lancaster, Pennsylvania

Printed and bound by LSC Communications,
Crawfordsville, Indiana

Designed by Casey Hampton